Early one morning, Tom and Twigs headed to the Branch Ranch. They'd heard that Ariela needed some help. "Howdy, Tom and Twigs! Thank goodness you boys are here," Ariela called when she saw them arriving.

"I've run out of Gummy Leaf and these beetles need to eat. I've got to herd them to the top field, and fast," Ariela told them.
"So do you want us to help you herd them?" Twigs asked. "We'd make great ranchers!"

Reacher Tom and the Baby Beetles

WE NEED TO TURN THE MAGIC ON,
WE NEED TO SAVE THE DAY.
COME ON!

BANTAM BOOKS

"Hello! Are you ready to come on another adventure in Treetopolis? First we need to do the moves that turn our magic powers on. Come on, join in!

TIME FOR TREE FU!

To make Tree Fu spells do what you see . . .
Slide to the side, and **jump** right back!
Hold your hands up high, **spin** around . . .
Reach up for the sky!

Look, the sapstone in my belt is **glowing**! Moving turned our magic on. Now we're ready!"

But Ariela just laughed and laughed!
"There's no way you two could be ranchers and herd these beetles. It's not easy, you know!" she replied. "The beetles need to trust you or they'll just run away. You'd never make it all the way to the top field!"

"So what *do* you want us to do, Ariela?" Tom asked.
"I'd like you to keep an eye on these three beetle eggs and make sure they're safe while I'm away. They're not due to hatch for a while yet," Ariela explained.

"Sounds **egg-stremely** easy!"
shrugged Tom and Twigs, still feeling a
bit sad that they couldn't be ranchers like Ariela.
"I'll bring some Gummy Leaf back for the baby beetles. They
have to eat soon after hatching or they'll be in big trouble!"
said Ariela, whistling to the beetles and then riding off on one
of their backs.

Left alone with the beetle eggs, Tom and Twigs decided to play a game of 'I spy' until Ariela returned. "I spy, with my little eye, something beginning with—"
Suddenly, they heard a scratching noise.
"Hey, it's the eggs!" Tom cried.
"They've hatched early!"

CRACK!

They rushed into the barn and found the baby beetles huddled together in a corner. "What's wrong with them, Tom?" Twigs wondered. "I guess they're hungry and want to see their mum and dad," Tom replied.

"Ariela said they need to eat soon after they hatch, so we're going to have to take them to the top field," Tom decided. "But Ariela said we couldn't. We're not ranchers!" Twigs reminded him. "Come on, Twigs, we can do this!" Tom laughed. "They're just babies. What could go wrong?"

Tom and Twigs had only just led the baby beetles out of the barn when they began to squeak loudly. Then they ran away across the fields, in the wrong direction.
"Stop! *Stop!*" Tom and Twigs quickly chased after them, flying through the air.

"They must be scared," Tom said, landing in front of the beetles so that they would have to stop. But it didn't work, they just kept running towards him.

"We've got to do something!" Twigs cried.

"Let's think. What would Ariela do?" Tom wondered.

Suddenly, Tom had an idea. "I know what to do!" he cried.
He whistled loudly, just like he'd heard Ariela doing outside the barn earlier. And it worked! The beetles stopped, and then began to walk slowly instead of running.

PHWEEE!

Tom and Twigs followed the beetles as they walked towards the top field, but soon Twigs' wings began to ache.
"Do you want to walk instead of flying?" Tom asked him.
"Then my feet will ache, too. Couldn't we just ride the beetles, like Ariela does?" Twigs wondered.
"Well, they'd have to trust us first," Tom told him.

THREE . . .

"How could they not trust this face?" Twigs grinned at Tom. Tom laughed. "OK then, let's try. One, two, three . . ." They both jumped onto the backs of the two bigger beetles. But the beetles didn't like it, throwing them off and then running towards a cornfield!

"Oh no!" Twigs gasped.
"It's OK, Twigs, we'll just whistle again and they'll come back," Tom said calmly.
"No, Tom, you don't understand! That's Thunder Popcorn!" Twigs told him.
And sure enough, they suddenly heard lots of loud popping sounds . . .

POP!

POP! POP! POP! POP! POP!

Huge pieces of popcorn began to explode everywhere. The beetles ran around the field, confused by the loud noises and flying popcorn. They were getting more and more scared by the minute.

"Poor little beetles! We have to help them!" Twigs cried.

"Right, we'll have to use **BIG WORLD MAGIC** to protect the baby beetles from the scary sounds of the Thunder Popcorn and get them out of this field. It's time to do the *Protecto Tunnel* spell. Are you ready?"

TREE FU GO!

"Copy me, into your spell pose."

"Kneel down on one knee, then kneel down on the other knee."

"Draw an arch up with your arms one way, over, then down."

"Draw an arch up with your arms the other way, over, then down."

"Crawl your hands out in front, then crawl your hands back."

"Draw arches up with both arms, and then down."

"Now clap and say 'Protecto Tunnel' to send the magic to me. Protecto Tunnel!"

"Yes, we did it! Thanks for your help!"

A glowing magic tunnel appeared, leading out of the field. Tom flew towards the beetles, rounding them into the tunnel. "Come on, guys, this will protect you from the noise and get you out of this field!" he told them.

THIS WAY!

Once they were out of the field and away from the popping noise, the beetles calmed down.
"That's better, isn't it?" Tom said quietly. Then, to his surprise, a beetle began nudging him.
"Wowzers! I think they want us to ride them," Twigs smiled, as he and Tom gently climbed on to the beetles' backs.

YEE HA!

"Yee ha!" cried Tom happily, as he and Twigs finally rode into the top field.

Ariela looked up in surprise. "Well I never! How did you get them up here?" she said, when she saw that the pair were riding on two of the baby beetles.

"With a lot of hard work!" said Twigs.
"And some trust, too," Tom added. "You
were right, Ariela, being a rancher isn't easy!"
"Yeah, but you did it! I was wrong before, you *are* ranchers
after all!" said Ariela. She then gave them both a star badge,
as the baby beetles ran to meet their parents.

Thanks for helping me in Treetopolis, see you soon for another adventure. Bye for now!

TREE
FU TOM: RANCHER
TOM AND THE BABY BEETLES
A BANTAM BOOK
978 0 857 51165 2

Published in Great Britain
by Bantam, an imprint of Random House
Children's Publishers UK
A Random House Group Company.

This edition published 2013

1 3 5 7 9 10 8 6 4 2

Tree Fu Tom created by Daniel Bays.
Based on the episode 'The Great Journey', written by Ian Carney.
TREE FU TOM word and device marks are trade marks of the British Broadcasting
Corporation and FremantleMedia Enterprises and are used under licence. TREE FU TOM
device marks © BBC and FremantleMedia Enterprises MMX. The "BBC" word mark and
logo are trade marks of the British Broadcasting Corporation and are used under licence.
BBC Logo © BBC 1996. Licensed by FremantleMedia Enterprises.

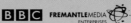

Bantam Books are published by Random House Children's Publishers UK,
61-63 Uxbridge Road, London W5 5SA

www.randomhousechildrens.co.uk

Addresses for companies within The Random House Group Limited can be found at:
www.randomhouse.co.uk/offices.htm

THE RANDOM HOUSE GROUP Limited Reg. No. 954009

A CIP catalogue record for this book is available
from the British Library

Printed in China

MIX
Paper from
responsible sources
FSC® C104723